2019 —
Merry Christmas
Kiri & Kia
Deborah Michlus
Author / Illustrator

This book is dedicated with love,
to my children, Jessica,
Bryan, and David, my strongest supporters.
Without their support, none of this would be possible

Published by Deborah Lockwood Micklus
© 2018 Deborah Lockwood Micklus
Text copyright © 1968 Deborah Lynn Lockwood
Illustration copyright
©1986, 1987, 2018 Deborah Lockwood Micklus

For information and permissions contact publisher.

First published in the United States by Deborah Lockwood Micklus
Distributed by IngramLight
ISBN 978-0-578-40604-6

The Perfect Christmas mistake

written & illustrated by Deborah Lockwood Micklus

A long while ago, before you were born, there was a small village nestled in a valley below a Great Palace. The kingdom was ruled by a cranky queen, Queen Isabella. Queen Isabella punished her people for the tiniest, pickiest, most ridiculous things!

The butcher was put in jail because his sausages were too skinny, the carpenter was jailed because his hammer was too loud, and the dressmaker was thrown in the dungeon because the queen's gown was too tight.

Queen Isabella had no patience for mistakes, and she never listened to anyone, but occasionally, she did listen to her daughter, Princess Amelia. Princess Amelia was gentle and kind, and always saw the good side of everything.

Christmas was one day that Queen Isabella wasn't as cranky as usual. On Christmas, people came from far away places to the Great Palace for the Christmas Feast.

They brought cakes, breads, candies and pies, sides of beef, whole turkeys, chickens, fish, pheasant, fruits and vegetables for The Christmas Feast, for all to enjoy.

One Christmas Eve, Fritz, the baker, and his apprentice, Claudio, worked into the long hours of the night preparing food for the Christmas Feast. Together they baked breads, pies, cookies, cakes and sweet candies.

The baker was not a
wealthy man. He was
just about out of
supplies, and wouldn't
have enough to finish
the queen's entire order.
He used the last bit of
sugar for the special
order red and green
candy sticks.
As always, there
were directions.

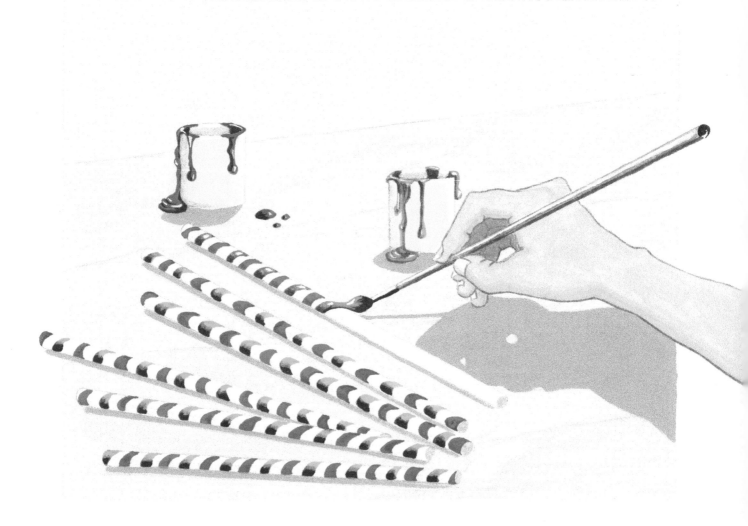

When the baker was finished preparing the candy mixture, Claudio pulled out pieces of the sticky mixture and rolled out long, thin sticks. He carefully painted each one, according to the queen's directions.

"As tall as a dinner knife,
no longer, no shorter
as wide as my pinky,
no fatter, no thinner
with ten stripes of red,
and ten stripes of green
make a mistake and
you'll answer to me!"

Finally, the baker and the apprentice went to bed. No sooner had they fallen asleep when downstairs a cabinet door opened slowly...

...and a tiny elf carefully peered out.

Deep underground, below the village, lived a colony of elves, in a maze of tunnels and small pockets cut from the earth. A plowed field, a scrubbed and shiny home, loaves of bread where there had been no wheat, were some of the surprises the villagers found from time to time.

Satisfied that all
was clear, the elf
pushed the door
open wider... and
THAT pushed
a bag of flour to
the floor, AND a
big mixing bowl,
a spoon, a knife,
and a heavy
rolling pin!

The little elf sprang to his feet, clasped his hands tightly together, and closing his eyes, wiggled his ears with all his might. Colored sparks flew through the air and... things began to happen!

The spilled flour rose up in a cloud and from it a cake appeared. From the mixing bowl came a plump loaf of bread, from a broken cup, hard candies in all colors, and from the rolling pin came twenty-one bread sticks! The room was filled with a whirlwind of colored sparks, clouds of flour, and sparkling grains of sugar.

Perhaps the elf's magic was too strong that night. Perhaps it was because it was Christmas Eve. The queen's entire order was magically finished. But the elf saw with a start that the special order candy sticks had been bent like little walking canes!

Suddenly, there was a loud thump as the apprentice awakened. There was no time to spare! The elf scrambled back into the cupboard, and hoped for the best.

Claudio hurried downstairs to pack all the goods for the Great Feast. He saw the sparkling kitchen, so many more candies, pies, and baked goods and was truly amazed! Queen Isabella's order was completely finished!

"Hurry now, Claudio," the baker called. "The queen doesn't take kindly to late-comers!"

Claudio quickly loaded the cart and returned to gather the special order candy sticks. His eyes popped out in surprise when he saw that each stick had been bent! He quickly packed them anyway, and started off to the palace. Through the small town, past houses, shops, and over the hills he went. He thought about the bent candy sticks and hoped for the best.

Inside the palace courtyard people bustled around unpacking and carrying their goods inside. Bowls of sumptuous fruits and vegetables, still steaming, sides of beef, huge rounds of cheese, beautiful pies, cakes, and candies. The palace maids were preparing the Great Hall for guests and the Great Presentation of Food.

High above all the busyness sat the elf. Perched upon the rafters, he watched people scurrying around as he looked for Claudio. Fritz, the baker, would be coming later.

A trumpet sounded announcing the Royal Family, and two huge doors opened as Queen Isabella and King Henry entered the room, followed by Princess Amelia.

Once seated, Queen Isabella clapped her hands, and commanded "Begin the Great Presentation at once!"

One by one, butchers, cooks, farmers, and bakers presented their special dishes to the queen. She looked down her long nose at each dish, nodded, and with a flick of her wrist beckoned the next in line. Then the apprentice stood before the queen.

"Have you brought the special order candy sticks?" She asked. "Yes, my queen," he whispered timidly.

Queen Isabella leaned closer. Something was not right. Suddenly her jaw dropped, her neck stretched out like a goose, and her eyes bulged! She snatched a candy from the plate and frowned, the deepest, most furious frown the kingdom had ever seen. Slowly she began, getting louder and louder:

"As tall as a dinner knife,
no longer, no shorter
as wide as my pinky,
no fatter, no thinner
with ten stripes of red,
and ten stripes of green
each special candy stick
was to have been!"

"Your M-M-Majesty…" Claudio stammered fearfully.

"You've made a mistake!" The queen shouted so loudly that the rafters began to shake. The walls began to tremble. The butchers, maids, cooks, farmers and bakers huddled together, afraid of the angry queen.

In the middle of all the commotion there was a loud plop, as the elf fell from the rafters landing in an apple-banana cake.

Everyone gasped. Claudio's hands flew up in surprise and the special order candy sticks went flying. All but one lay shattered at the queen's feet.

The elf held the one remaining unbroken candy. Princess Amelia sprang from her throne, and ran to the fallen elf. She stared at the candy he held, and she smiled.

"What a perfect candy for Christmas!" She cried, "A candy cane!" Princess Amelia politely asked the tiny elf if she could hold it.

The elf was delighted and held out the candy to the princess. As soon as she touched it he disappeared.

A hush came over the Great Hall. The princess stepped lightly to the Christmas tree, shining with candles and decorations. She gently hung the candy from a bough and smiled.

"Sometimes the most beautiful things happen quite by mistake," she said to no one in particular.

Queen Isabella thought about this. She thought about the butcher, the carpenter, and the dressmaker. She saw the candy sparkling from the bough of the tree, and thought maybe Amelia was right. Everyone makes mistakes. And sometimes they turn out to be perfect.

She smiled, then announced loudly so everyone in the hall could hear, "Release the prisoners! Bring them in to the Great Hall. The Candy Cane shall be part of Christmas forever! It is the perfect Christmas mistake!

CPSIA information can be obtained
at www.ICGtesting.com
Printed in the USA
LVHW011031211218
601105LV00001B/8/P